Real Stuck, Way Up

Benette W. Tiffault
Illustrated by Sher Sester

BARRON'S

DEDICATION
For my Eli

All inquiries should be addressed to:
Barron's Educational Series, Inc.
250 Wireless Boulevard
Hauppauge, New York 11788

International Standard Book No. 0-8120-9166-3

Library of Congress Catalog Card No. 94-44593

Library of Congress Cataloging-in-Publication Data

Tiffault, Benette W.
    Real stuck, way up / by Benette W. Tiffault ; illustrated by
Sher Sester.
        p. cm.
    Summary: A cumulative tale in which many objects are used
unsuccessfully to try to knock an apple down from a tree.
    ISBN 0-8120-9166-3
    [1. Trees—Fiction.]   I. Sester, Sher, ill. II. Title.
PZ7.T452Re 1995
[E]—dc20
                                   94-44593
                                     CIP
                                     AC

PRINTED IN HONG KONG
5678 9955 987654321

There once was an apple
I wanted to bite,
but the apple was stuck,
real stuck, way up,
in the middle
of the apple tree.

So . . .
I tossed up my ball
to knock down the apple,
but the ball got stuck,
real stuck, way up,
in the middle
of the apple tree.

So...
I tossed up my shoe
to kick the ball,
to knock down the apple,
but my shoe got stuck,
real stuck, way up,
in the middle
of the apple tree.

So . . .

I tossed up my glove

to slap my shoe,

to kick my ball,

to knock down the apple,

but my glove got stuck,

real stuck, way up,

in the middle

of the apple tree.

So . . .
I tossed up my rope
to lasso my glove,

to slap my shoe,

to kick my ball,

to knock down the apple,

but my rope got stuck,

real stuck, way up,

in the middle

of the apple tree.

So . . .

I tossed up my truck
to pull my rope,
to lasso my glove,
to slap my shoe,
to kick my ball,
to knock down the apple,
but my truck got stuck,
real stuck, way up,
in the middle
of the apple tree.

So . . .

I tossed up my racquet
to smack my truck,
to pull my rope,
to lasso my glove,
to slap my shoe,
to kick my ball,
to knock down the apple,
but my racquet got stuck,
real stuck, way up,
in the middle
of the apple tree.

S_o...

I tossed up my umbrella
to poke my racquet,
to smack my truck,
to pull my rope,
to lasso my glove,
to slap my shoe,
to kick my ball,
to knock down the apple,
but my umbrella got stuck,
real stuck, way up,
in the middle
of the apple tree.

So...

I tossed up my bowling pin
to strike my umbrella,
to poke my racquet,
to smack my truck,
to pull my rope,
to lasso my glove,
to slap my shoe,
to kick my ball,
to knock down the apple,
but my bowling pin got stuck,
real stuck, way up,
in the middle
of the apple tree.

So . . .
I tossed up my bat
to bop my bowling pin,
to strike my umbrella,
to poke my racquet,
to smack my truck,
to pull my rope,
to lasso my glove,
to slap my shoe,
to kick my ball,
to knock down the apple,
but my bat got stuck,
real stuck, way up,
in the middle
of the apple tree.

So . . .
I climbed up that tree,
way up, up high,
to the top, tippy top
of the apple tree.
Then I shimmied and shook
and to my delight . . .

I rattled my bat

that bopped my bowling pin,

that struck my umbrella,

that poked my racquet,

that smacked my truck,

that pulled my rope,

that lassoed my glove,

that slapped my shoe,

that kicked my ball . . .

and there everything was,

unstuck, right there,

way down beneath

the apple tree.

But now I was stuck,
real stuck, way up,
in the middle of the apple tree.

So . . .
I sat myself down
and took a big bite
of the apple I plucked
from a branch way up
in the middle of the apple tree.

The End